Ayudantes de la comunidad / Helping the Community

¿Qué hacen LOS RECOLECTORES DE BASURA?
What Do GARBAGE COLLECTORS Do?

Richard Alexander

Traducido por Eida de la Vega

PowerKiDS press
New York

Published in 2016 by The Rosen Publishing Group, Inc.
29 East 21st Street, New York, NY 10010

First Edition

Editor: Katie Kawa
Book Design: Katelyn Heinle
Spanish Translator: Eida de la Vega

Photo Credits: Cover (garbage collector), pp. 1, 13 Don Mason/Blend Images/Getty Images; cover (hands) bymandesigns/Shutterstock.com; back cover Zffoto/Shutterstock.com; p. 5 360b/Shutterstock.com; p. 6 Dmitry Kalinovsky/Shutterstock.com; p. 9 Johnny Habell/Shutterstock.com; p. 10 © iStockphoto.com/kozmoat98; pp. 14, 17, 18 © iStockphoto.com/PeopleImages; pp. 21, 24 (landfill) yevgeniy11/Shutterstock.com; p. 22 © iStockphoto.com/whitemay; p. 24 (garbage) Nataliya Hora/Shutterstock.com.

Library of Congress Cataloging-in-Publication Data

Alexander, Richard, author.
What do garbage collectors do? = ¿Qué hacen los recolectores de basura? / Richard Alexander.
pages cm. — (Helping the community = Ayudantes de la comunidad)
Parallel title: Ayudantes de la comunidad.
In English and Spanish.
Includes bibliographical references and index.
ISBN 978-1-4994-0611-5 (library binding)
1. Sanitation workers—Juvenile literature. 2. Refuse and refuse disposal—Juvenile literature. I. Title.
HD8039.S257A44 2016
628.4'42—dc23

Manufactured in the United States of America

CPSIA Compliance Information: Batch #WS15PK: For Further Information contact Rosen Publishing, New York, New York at 1-800-237-9932

CONTENIDO

CONTENTS

Los recolectores de **basura** trabajan muy duro.

Garbage collectors work very hard.

Mantienen limpias las ciudades.

They keep our towns clean.

Los recolectores de basura recogen la basura. La gente deja la basura en basureros cerca de la calle.

Garbage collectors pick up garbage. People leave their garbage in cans near the street.

Los recolectores de basura echan la basura en un camión grande.

Garbage collectors put the garbage into a big truck.

Un trabajador maneja
el camión.

One worker drives the truck.

Otros trabajadores recogen la basura.

Other workers pick up the garbage.

Los trabajadores a veces viajan parados en la parte de atrás del camión.

The workers sometimes stand on the back of the truck as it moves.

Los trabajadores usan ropa de colores brillantes para que los automovilistas los vean.

The workers wear bright colors so drivers can see them.

Llevan la basura a un **vertedero**. Este es un lugar donde hay mucha basura.

They take the garbage to a **landfill**. This is a place with a lot of garbage.

¡Los recolectores de basura hacen un trabajo importante!

Garbage collectors have an important job to do!

PALABRAS QUE DEBES APRENDER
WORDS TO KNOW

(la) basura
garbage

(el) vertedero
landfill

ÍNDICE / INDEX

SITIOS DE INTERNET / WEBSITES

Due to the changing nature of Internet links, PowerKids Press has developed an online list of websites related to the subject of this book. This site is updated regularly. Please use this link to access the list: www.powerkidslinks.com/htc/gcol